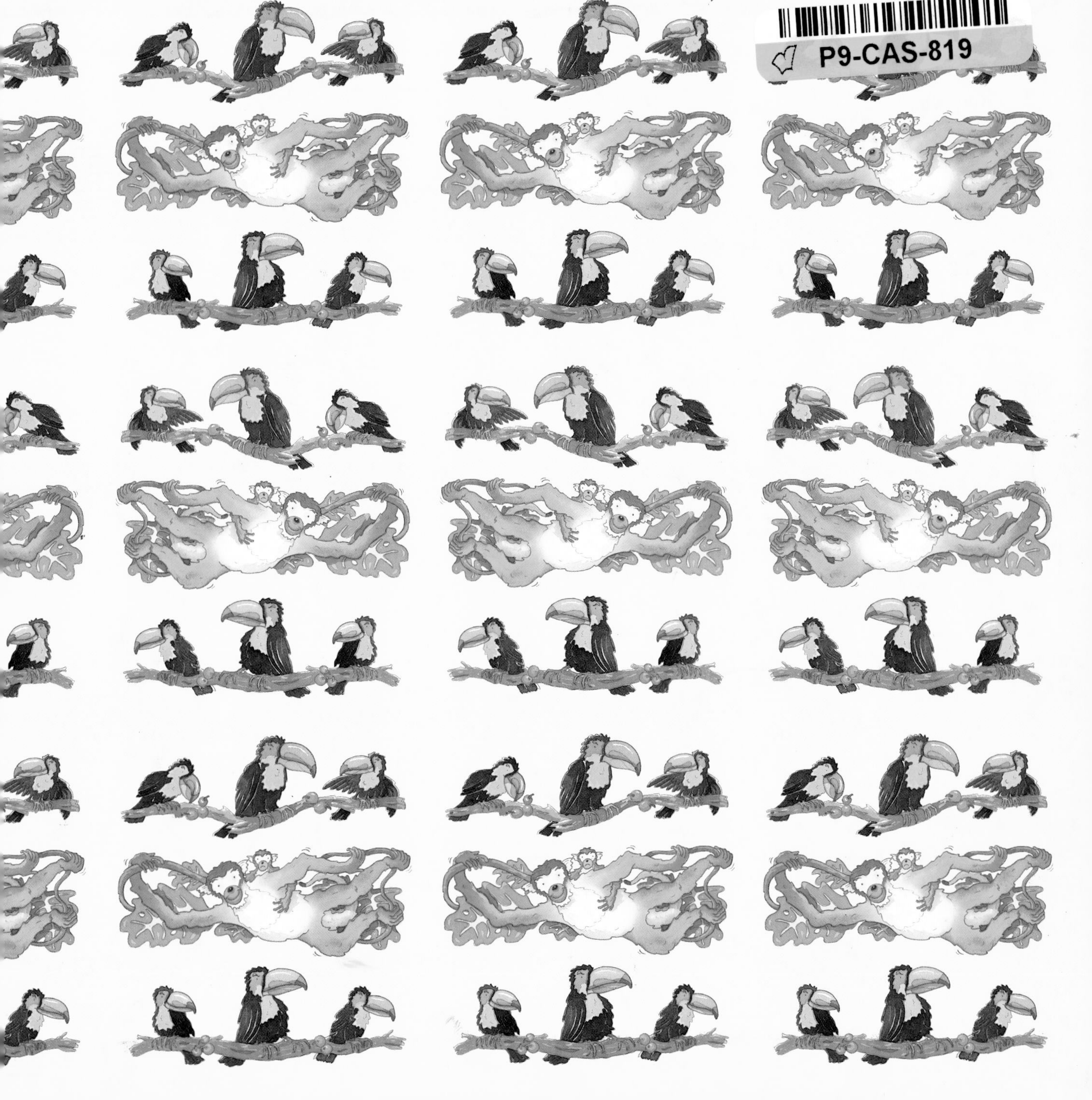

For Josephine

BLACKIE CHILDREN'S BOOKS
Published by the Penguin Group
Penguin Books Ltd, 27 Wrights Lane, London W8 5TZ, England
Penguin Books Australia Ltd, Ringwood, Victoria, Australia
Penguin Books Canada Ltd, 10 Alcorn Avenue, Toronto, Ontario, Canada M4V 3B2
Penguin Books (NZ) Ltd, 182–190 Wairau Road, Auckland 10, New Zealand

Penguin Books Ltd, Registered Offices: Harmondsworth, Middlesex, England

First published in 1993
10 9 8 7 6 5 4 3 2 1
First edition
Text copyright © 1993 Emma Guénier
Illustrations copyright © 1993 Jonathan Satchell

The moral right of the author and illustrator has been asserted

A CIP catalogue record for this book is available from the British Library

ISBN 0 216 940125

First American edition published in 1993 by
Peter Bedrick Books
2112 Broadway
New York, NY 10023

Library of Congress Cataloging-in-Publication Data is available for this title

ISBN 0–87226–512–9

Filmset in Futura Book

Made and printed in Hong Kong

IN THE WILD

Jonathan Satchell • Emma Guénier

Bedrick/Blackie
New York

Blackie
London

Many animals live in the wild.
Who lives in the grass?

Who lives in the tree?

Who lives by the river?

Who lives on the snow?

Who lives in the cave?

How many wild animals
can you count?